TRUTH & TRYSTS

The Innocence of the Iris

By Donna Valenti

D1528437

DEDICATION:

This book is dedicated to anyone who has ever been attracted to the beauty of the Iris.

TRUTH & TRYSTS

The Innocence of the Iris

By Donna Valenti

PREFACE

I don't think much is left to chance in life. I believe that most circumstances are serendipitous, at the very least. I believe we are guided by a combination of God and our gut. This is what experience and hindsight have taught me. In life, we come full circle, sometimes more than once, and when we realize the adjoining point at which our journey began and where it has ended, we must recognize that point because doing so ensures the start of a new journey; it ensures that we take a tangent.

But we must write it (the journey) down for the sake of edification and purification, for the sake of a new beginning. That is the motivation for this publication.

ACKNOWLEDGEMENT:

To my family and friends who have supported me in pursuit of my dream and to Chloe for appearing at the right time in order to make this dream a reality.

We are of different opinions
At different hours but we
Always may be said to be at
Heart on the same side of Truth

Ralph Waldo Emerson

Chapter 1

My Sweet Sixteen party took place at the end of April, in the year 1987. Everything was pink that day; I wouldn't hear of any other color. My dress was pink. My mother made it, as she had made all of my other dresses in the years before. Her favorite one, or I should say her favorite story about the dresses she made for me was the one she told about my First Communion dress. She made me a white eyelet dress, but I wanted one of the nylon ones that pervaded all of the department stores. When the dress was finished, I still insisted that I wanted to wear one of the nylon ones. My mother became distraught; she felt guilty for making me miserable. Not knowing what to do, my mother appealed to my second grade teacher, Mrs. Flanagan, for advice. Mrs. Flanagan absolved my mother of any intimations of "child abuse" and told her to make me wear that dress.

But I was happy about my Sweet Sixteen dress from beginning to end. It was a strapless dress, whose body was made of pink satin that appeared almost white after my mother added the layers of tulle to it. The tulle of the bodice was sheared and fitted. The bodice traveled to a stop at the left side of my waist, but on my right side, continued a bit farther at an angle to my hip. The skirt of the dress reached just above my knees in three, four, maybe five layers of tulle. The dress was beautiful. It was feminine.

I wore pink that day because pink typifies Sweet Sixteen's. It seems to me that colors characterize the stages of our lives: blue for baby boys and sad times, pink for baby girls and Sweet Sixteen's, yellow roses for friendship, red roses for passionate evenings, green for envy and black for funerals.

But colors confuse the stages of our lives too. That's what happened to me on the day of my First Communion. First Communions are associated with white -but then so are weddings. On the day of my First Communion, I imagined myself a bride. It wasn't that I had confused the Third Sacrament with the Fifth, or that anyone had failed to explain the difference to me in religion class. It wasn't even sacrilege. It simply was that, on that day, I wore a white dress and a white veil. I walked down the aisle with a boy from my class. While my religious instructions prepared me for a blessing of the Lord, while I was told I would soon partake of one of God's greatest miracles for the first time, I was still a seven year-old child whose imagination betrayed my innocence through no fault of anyone's. Or was it that my innocence betrayed my imagination?

Anyway, as I have grown, my imagination has continued to betray my innocence. Only now, it often betrays what some people might call ignorance. Like the time during my tenth grade chemistry class, when Dr. Gross was busy explaining the "Big Bang" theory, and I interrupted him and naively asked: "Wait, but this is the scientific view, right?" revealing my religious indoctrination and presumably gullible disposition. Dr. Gross chuckled as he said, "Yes," revealing his atheistic bias. That is one of the unfortunate plights of maturity: We exchange innocence for ignorance.

Ever since then, my imagination fosters what some people would call "hypotheses" or "conjectures." Now, "innocent-less" but "wonder-filled," I imagine that God exists and that God does not exist. I speculate. I question. I doubt. I imagine because I wonder, and I wonder because I think. And it's not the having had a religious background, or the not having had a religious background, but the wonder, the intellect, that leads me to my imaginings.

That is now.

But then, on the night of my Sweet Sixteen, my thoughts were narrowly restricted to the success of my party. So, I recited the rosary on my fingers in the bathtub. After all, it was supposed to rain. I prayed that my party would be a success. It rained, and it was.

I respect faith,
but doubt is what gets you an
education.

Wilson Mizner

Chapter 2

I met him the next night at someone else's Sweet Sixteen party. Prior to that night, I hadn't known him except for the fact that he was intimidating in class. He used to yell "Excellent!" from the back of the classroom when he understood something and murmur under his breath when others didn't.

Then there was that time in ninth grade biology class when we were watching one of those science films that's usually narrated by some guy with an accent. I think this particular one was about butterflies. Well anyway, when we finally got a look at the guy talking, he jumped up from the back of the classroom, pointed and yelled: "Hey, that's my uncle!" We were all stunned, especially the teacher. He swore he was telling the truth. He said, "Go ask my sister if you don't believe me." His sister was a senior in the same school at the time.

He asked me for my phone number that night at the party with almost as much fervor. He never struck me as my type before. I had previously paired myself with boys who adopted the preppy look more often associated with the 80's. But he wore his hair long in the back and he wore Metalhead T-shirts. He wasn't all that tall either. He was only five feet and six inches. His nose was crooked too. He had broken it two or three times while wrestling. It had never occurred to him to get it fixed -or maybe he had just refused to undergo "cosmetic" surgery because he loathed artificiality. He was bowlegged too.

My mother once told me a story about my grandfather and a bowlegged woman. It goes likes this: When my grandfather was still living in Italy, he was engaged to marry a woman he'd never encountered before. He didn't object to the marriage until, one day, he noticed her walking down the street and saw that she was bowlegged. It was then that he refused to marry her. However shallow this may sound, my grandfather was a wise man. When my mother stood in front of her closet as a teenager, trying to decide what to wear on any given weekend, my grandfather would say to her, "If you had only one dress, you would know what to wear." Perhaps, I should have exercised the same precaution that my 'grandfather did in choosing a love interest. After all, my grandfather didn't marry the bowlegged woman, and he came to America instead. Perhaps I, too, would have arrived at a different shore sooner. But I didn't. My journey took longer than my grandfather's, and he even had to take a detour through Canada.

He stood next to the front door, as I was about to leave the party. He leaned his head and body on his elbow that rested upon the wall next to the front door. The other arm hung by his side with his plaid flannel shirt in hand.

6

He wore a blue thermal T-shirt. His raised arm unabashedly revealed that he had been perspiring. But, I don't know, maybe I gave him my phone number because of the way he carried a conversation with me earlier in the evening, while holding his legs and feet over his head with his hands in a somersault stance, even though we both knew he hadn't been drinking. Eccentricity came naturally to him. Being normal would prove to be a struggle.

Chapter 3

He called me the next night, a Sunday night. He told me that he vacationed in Nova Scotia every summer. He loved it there. He said that he had learned to windsurf there. I was impressed. In turn, I informed him that my family and I had been camping since I was three years old.

"In a tent or a trailer?" he asked.

"In a tent," I answered.

"Cool. None of those false senses of security like T.V. and a microwave. Hey, do you jog?" he wanted to know.

"No, I don't jog, but I exercise at least four or five times a week," I offered.

"Hey, I hope you're not one of those people who jogs on a treadmill in a gym or rides a stationary bike. That just kills the whole experience... the whole point of it... being outdoors." As I said, he loathed artificiality.

But I did exercise indoors -to Jane Fonda's exercise video, no less, so I changed the subject. "When you called, I was in the middle of reading *The Scarlet Letter* for my American Literature class."

"Cool. Do you like it?" he asked.

"Yeah, I guess it's all right," I replied.

"So what do you like to read?" he probed.

"Well, I like to read almost anything. I will read anything, but right now I prefer the Russian novelists for their 'l'angoisse.'"

"Hey, isn't that a French term?"

"Yeah."

"So, you like to read."

"Oh, yeah, I love it. For years, books kept me company while everyone went off to summer camp."

"Well, me too. I like to read too. Sometimes, I read two or three books at a time. When I'm in Nova Scotia, I like to climb on a roof and read. I like to be as alone as possible with an author, his imagination, and mine." I was smiling on my end of the phone. I was surprised to find that we had something in common, particularly reading.

Then, he said, "You know what else is great in this world besides a good jog and a good book? A good hug. Yeah, I like hugs."

"Well, I happen to have a poem on hugs. I'll bring it to school tomorrow for you."

"That sounds great. I'll see you tomorrow, then."

"O.K."

"Donna?"

"Yes?"

"If you don't ever feel like shaving your legs or forget or something, don't worry about it."

"O.K.," I said, a bit perplexed. I had no intentions of doing either.

"Goodnight."

"Goodnight."

Chapter 4

Soon after I gave him the poem on hugs, he gave me a short story, the meaning and relevance of which neither of us fully understood at the time.

He was currently enrolled in an English class with Mrs. Mayers. He used to sit in the fourth or fifth seat from the front, and in the row closest to the windows. He didn't like that class. "Too many religious allusions," he'd said. I knew what he was talking about because I had read *Lord of The Flies* with Mrs. Mayers the semester before in a different class. But I really did think that Simon was a Christ figure. He didn't. I learned that he was an atheist. So, it wasn't unusual that one afternoon, instead of paying attention in class, he was reading from a book of short stories by Hermann Hesse that he had pulled from off the shelves next to him. He opened the book to a story titled "Iris." When he finished reading it, he tore the same story out of the book and then he gave it to me. I took it home and read it, myself. This is a summary of Hesse's story:

In his childhood, Anselm used to play in the garden. His favorite flower was also his mother's favorite flower, the Iris. Anselm was in the habit of staring into the flower's mouth, its abyss, which held heart and thoughts, breath and dreams. In the budding flower,

Anselm, himself a growing child, espied the unfolding of its thoughts and dreams from the abyss. The Iris spoke to Anselm and advised him that the world is worth contemplating, worth marveling at. The flower invited him to explore the interior of the world. Questions emerged from the opening flower, and Anselm's soul dove inside of it in anticipation of answers. In it, Anselm began to discover the interconnectedness of things. Anselm became preoccupied with the relationship between himself and the outside world. He was exploring the mystery of childhood.

But seasons came and went, and Anselm developed other interests outside of the flower, outside of sounds and smells. Anselm grew physically. He suffered through secondary school and college. He traveled to distant lands and on great ships. In the eyes of others, he became an unpredictable eccentric. Anselm's soul had taken a detour. He no longer saw God and eternity dwelling in the depths of the blue Iris, as he had before in his childhood. Routinely, Anselm returned from his journeys dissatisfied and disconnected. Suddenly, Anselm remembered and visited a friend's sister, whose name was Iris, though the name itself meant nothing to him at first. Such was his despair. Anselm grew connected to her name, to her, wondering what there was for him behind them both. Anselm wanted to marry Iris and expressed his desire to her; but sensing his unrest and examining the furrows in his forehead, Iris gave him a task to complete instead of granting him her acceptance. Iris, who knew as well as Anselm, that her name represented something lost and forgotten in his life, set him on a search to uncover it.

In the midst of his journey, Iris died, but she left him a sign. She gave him a blue Iris before passing on. Still, not until a winter's day, when he was walking through the snow in an open field, ice forming on his beard, did he come upon a single Iris and did he remember. With remembrance, came recognition. Anselm recognized once again his childhood, his soul, eternity, God, himself and the Truth. Anselm finally entered the mystery and the light.

He had written on the pages of the story. He had underlined words and sentences with his pen. He wrote questions to Hesse -or were they to himself? Or maybe even to me? I wasn't quite sure. Then, finally, on the bottom of the last page, he wrote:

Is life just composed of pictures as Hesse describes it, and through these pictures is it possible to attain true life of the spirit? Do you have to give up the life of the senses completely in order to achieve the life of the spirit? Is being appointed professor, getting doctorates, graduating degrees, studying nights, only to achieve another "picture," "life," (was it all) or is life something more, something that comes from within? Why must it be this way?

I was intrigued by the thoughts he had expressed, and I was touched by the fact that he had bestowed them upon me.

Chapter 5

I grew up in a conservative household. My mother worked as a home typist until I entered the seventh grade. However, I found myself alone a lot in the evenings this particular spring of my sophomore year of high school. My brother was a senior in our high school and out a lot with his friends. My parents, for their part, were consumed with the plans for his graduation and for his prom. It is a long-standing tradition in our small town for the parents to assemble and collaborate on the senior prom or, as we call it, the Gambol. The local merchants donate funds while the parents collate their creative skills and enormous energy in order to transform the high school gym into an elaborate imitation of any one of an assortment of places: New York City, Paris, the Taj-Mahal, etc. The theme changes from year to year.

One of these evenings during the week, toward the end of May, he appeared unexpectedly at my front door with a blue Iris in his hands. Immediately, I looked inside of it, smelled it, and thanked him. Since I was alone in the house, I invited him in. I walked toward my bedroom door and he followed me into my room, closing the door behind us. I sat down on the edge of my bed, and so did he, in such a way that we were facing the mirror that hung above my dresser. I moved the Iris to my nose again so that all that I could see of my features in the mirror were my eyes. My eyes met his in the mirror and I looked down and away. Then, I lay down on my bed, eyes fixed on the ceiling. By now, he was lying alongside of me so that his upper body weight rested on one elbow, eyes on me. He reached down and kissed my lips.

"You're afraid to look at me or something," he said.

"Yes."

"Yes, what?"

"Yes, I'm afraid."

He reached his hand to my stomach and I flinched.

"I'm sorry, I just can't relax," I told him.

Then, he reached his hand to my left arm. I was wearing a T-shirt. He ran his fingers along my left arm, up and down. Then, after some time, he ran his fingers along the right one. Then, he reached his hand to my leg. I was wearing shorts. He ran his fingers along the left one first and then the right one. Then, he reached his fingers to my mouth. They lingered there until he moved them to my stomach again.

All the while, his touch wasn't the kind that would excite you to passion, but the kind that soothes, relaxes and reassures. In fact, I was feeling sleepy. He must have been feeling sleepy too because, after some time, he lay his head on my stomach and left it there.

That's when we heard my dad come through the front door. He jumped up and so did I. He hid behind the side of my bookcase while I walked out of my bedroom and into the kitchen. I was on a mission; I wanted to see if my dad had plans of going to sleep any time soon. However, the first thing I noticed was that the TV had been turned on, the newspaper was wide open, and there was an empty cup waiting to be filled with coffee. I said something to my dad about needing a glass of water and then went back to my room.

He left through my bedroom window that night and walked all the way home, as he explained to me the next day with a sense of delight and adventure.

Chapter 6

In the time that we were spending together, I was learning more and more things about him. I learned that his father was a social worker and his mother was an English teacher. His sister was in her freshman year of college by now. She worked at a gas station and she was the owner of two pet snakes. They had a dog, named Plato, and none of them thought it was at all necessary to close the bathroom doors. They were not modest; they were liberals.

He, himself, collected comic books, read his biology book for "fun," liked to climb trees, and often washed his feet in the kitchen sink.

He didn't live far from school. So, one afternoon, he brought me back to his house and took me into the dining room. In silence, he set up a slide projector on the table. There was no need for a screen. The blank white wall did the job. He said that the slides he was going to show me were of Nova Scotia, Canada. He explained that his mother's side of the family owned a great deal of property there. The property had been handed down from a famous American inventor, who, likewise, was his great-grandfather. I remember just one slide. It was a picture of him, his sister and his cousin. They all had their arms around one another. I don't remember any of the others because he had hardly begun, when he stopped. One minute, he was excited to show me the slides, and the next minute, he just shut the machine off. Then he said, "I can't believe I'm showing you this." He was embarrassed. He had lost himself to the moment, to nostalgia, to his excitement, and I was touched yet again.

One of the things that always attracted me to him was that he would lose himself to his emotions. He would just let go, whether it was excitement or frustration that would overcome him. It was precisely these two emotions, excitement and frustration, that contributed the most to his disposition. He could rarely hold a thought or an expression. It was a matter of urgency with him. It was such a natural thing -such a human thing. He was always bursting.

The funny thing is that I was actually interested in seeing those slides, in hearing about Nova Scotia; but I didn't say so. I just watched as he put the slide projector away.

Chapter 7

He introduced me to the Sands Point Preserve on a Saturday afternoon the last weekend in May. Located on Middleneck Road, tall, black wrought iron gates open up into a long concrete road. The road travels over a bridge (no water) for about fifty feet and then the bridge becomes a road again. The road leads to a field of grass.

We walked across the field of grass to the Castle Gould and around the circumference of the castle. He gave me a tour. He considered a person's value to be commensurate with a person's knowledge because he came from a family of doctors, writers, teachers, scientists and one very famous inventor. I, for my part, considered the value of a person's life commensurate with his/ her knowledge because I did not come from a family of doctors, writers, teachers, scientists or inventors. I came from a family of more recent immigrant status and of laborers. I was starving for the many conversations we would have.

"The Castle Gould," he began, "was built in 1912 by Howard Gould, a railroad heir. It was modeled after a Tudor house in England. It has eighty-eight rooms. Gould had built it for his fiancé, whom he never married, so he ended up selling it to the Guggenheims. The Guggenheims lived in the place until 1930, I think."

The castle had a tower. I told him that it reminded me of the one described in Henry James' novel, *Turn of The Screw*. He had had the same thought, he told me. Then, he told me that the tower was sixty feet tall. But he wasn't finished with his lesson yet; he continued: "After her husband's death, Mrs. Guggenheim sold the property to The Institute of Aeronautical Sciences, but that was after the castle was home to European, refugee children for a couple of years. And then, in 1946, the U.S. Navy bought the property and used it as a Training Devices Center. In 1967, it closed and the property was deeded to Nassau County."

Then, he took my hand and we walked back across the green field and toward the Hempstead House, where the stables once were. Now, however, the Hempstead House was a museum. At the moment, it featured a Dinosaur exhibit.

Then, we walked back across the green field and sat down under a tree near the picnic benches. Then, he told me that he would take me to Falaise one day. Falaise was the home of the Guggenheims' son, Captain Harry Guggenheim. The captain had lived there with his wife, the daughter of Teddy Roosevelt's secretary of the navy. The Captain had friends like Frank Lloyd Wright and Charles Lindbergh, who often visited him there. In fact,

Lindbergh had written his book titled, *We,* in that very same house.

When we finally stopped walking and he stopped talking about the factual information, I lay down on my back and closed my eyes.

That's when he lay down on the grass too, before turning on his side. He took a maple leaf seed in his fingers. He opened it up and stuck it on his nose.

"My sister and I used to wear these things on our noses all the time in Nova Scotia," he said.

After I opened my eyes to look at it as best as I could, I told him that my brother and I used to do the same thing.

"I guess all kids do," he said, with disappointment. He hated to be reminded that he was just like everybody else.

I was so sleepy; I yawned. As I did, he stuck his finger in my mouth and said, "Watch out for the flies." We laughed. He loved to demand attention, even if he didn't know he did. Then, he looked down at me and said, "You're beautiful."

"Thank you," I said, and then I reached up and kissed him. I was thanking him for his compliment, as well as his knowledge of and curiosity about things.

The Preserve. It was a place to go visit a museum, explore an old castle, find trees and stretch out on a field of grass. It was a place to go.

Not much later, I developed a case of mononucleosis. He didn't come visit me -having him sit at the edge of my bed and feed me chicken soup wasn't appropriate behavior for two sixteen-year-olds who had just started dating -but he sent me a card. On the outside, the cover bore a picture of a rainbow and it said:

Sunny thoughts to cheer you because you're special
On the inside, he drew a bleeding heart and wrote:
My heart bleeds the longer i'm away from you.
He never capitalized his i's when he wrote.
"Special and beautiful."
He often called me special and beautiful. Those two words used to fill me up.

I recovered about two weeks later, and, by that time, we were nearing the end of June and the end of the school year. The summer was beginning. Soon, he'd be leaving for wrestling camp in Minneapolis, where he'd spend a month, and then he'd head for Nova Scotia for the remainder of the summer. The only thing that would keep him home for a little while longer was a wrestling program in town that would last for a week.

In that time, we went to see the film, *A Room With a View*, one Friday night the third weekend in June.

Before the movie, he said he thought I'd like it. I did. Afterwards, we sat outside in front of his house. I sat on their picnic table and he sat on one of the benches facing me with his hands on my knees.

He asked me, "Did you mind the nudity?"

"No, but that's the first time I'd seen nude men on film."

"And?"

"And nothing. It's just that that was the first time..."

"What?"

"What do you mean 'what? You know what."

"Say it. I want to hear you say it."

"Why?"

"Because you don't look me in the eyes. Because you're shy about it."

"I know I am. I can't help it. Sometimes, the intensity in your eyes is too much for me. I get embarrassed."

"So just say it. Get it out and get it over with."

"No. I can't. I told you."

"Then forget me. Talk about you."

"What about me?"

"What would you call that?" he asked looking between my knees.

"No, I can't say it."

"Yes, you can. Just say what you're thinking. What are you thinking about?"

"An Iris," I said, and he smiled.

We had just two more days in town before he would leave for Minneapolis. On that day, my phone rang early in the morning. When I picked up the phone, he told me that he wasn't going to attend his last day of camp, not to make any plans, to go back to sleep, but to call him as soon as I woke up. It was eleven o'clock when I called him -three hours since he'd called.

"I'm so sorry," I apologized. "I didn't expect to wake up so much later. I thought I'd only sleep another hour or so. You probably should have called me back."

"That's O.K. Forget about it."

"What have you been doing? Did you go back to sleep too?"

"Nah, I've been walking around the house singing that song from *Hair*... 'Oh Donna, Oh Oh Donna, I'm looking for my Donna, my sixteen-year-old virgin...'"

"Are you making that up?"

"You mean you've never seen it?"

"No."

"That's too bad. Good show. Downright cultural and historical."

That day, we spent a couple of hours at the Preserve. We walked down toward the beach and along the water. He broke the silence somewhat awkwardly, though purposefully.

"In that show, *Hair*, they get naked. Everyone got naked in the '60's."

"Yeah?" I asked uneasily.

"Hey, would you ever go skinny dipping?" he asked.

"No, certainly not in broad daylight. Besides, isn't it the 80's?"

"I do it all the time in Canada. My cousins and I... we don't care."

"I would never do that with my cousins."

"Why? Don't you think of the body as natural?"

"Yes, but..."

"What about sex?"

"What about sex?!"

"Would you do that?"

"Not now."

"When?"

"When I'm married."

"What?! Why?!"

"Because I'm not supposed to."

"Says who?"

"God and my mother. "

He didn't offer a rebuttal; I mistook this respite as a sign of respect, a sign of restraint.

26

In his bedroom an hour or two later, I stood before him as he took off every article of clothing I had been wearing. Showing continued restraint, he paused to fold them neatly on his desk. I was fully naked before him for the first time, and soon, so was he. He removed his own clothing as I stood opposite him and watched.

Then, he took my hand and led me to his mattress on the floor, where he kissed my lips, my neck and my breasts. My eyes were closed shut, like someone fearing an oncoming train. I couldn't relax.

Then, as yet another sign of restraint, he lay down next to me. Our legs caressed one another. He took my hand in his and he squeezed it. I opened my eyes. That had been it, for a little while, anyway.

Some time later, we were still in his room, though fully clothed, when his father came home from work. His father knocked on the closed and suspicious door. When he opened it, he was surprised to see us sitting on the floor sharing a book. His father said hello to me and then to him, he said, "So, you stayed home today...?" He didn't sound angry, just surprised.

"Yeah," he answered his father.

Then, his father turned and said to me, 'Wow, he missed a tournament today. He's never done that before."

"Shh," he said to his father.

"Oh, you didn't know? He didn't tell you?"

"No," I said.

I admired him for three things that day: the sacrifice he had made, the feelings it had betrayed, and the nobility with which he had made it.

The following evening, I went out to dinner with him and his family. We ate some Greek food at a locally acclaimed restaurant. After dinner, he and I took a walk around Baxter Pond. During our lap around the pond, we paused to sit down on one of the many benches.

"Whenever my sister and my parents would have a fight, my sister would come here and I would run after her," he said.

We sat there in silence for a while, holding each other's hands. I was remembering how I had been surprised when I met his sister, Laurel, for the first time. I was surprised by how normal she looked. I was surprised because I never knew her when she was in the same high school, but I did know of her best friend, Mackenzie, who was a hippie. She was weird. They both behaved like hippies when hippies were no longer the "thing" to be. Oh sure, kids in our school wore tied dyed T-shirts, *Birkenstocks*, and smoked pot, but they owned *Coach* pocketbooks. And yet, Laurel had been wearing large, silver hoop earrings the first time I met her, which is something I would have worn. But still, I never would have worked in a gas station or owned pet snakes, like her.

After some time, we walked back to his house. Suddenly, he stopped me. He wrapped his arms around my back and held me so suddenly and tightly that my elbows were locked at a right angle between my chest and his; my hands were resting on his shoulders. Our eyes were locked too.

And then he said, "I think I love you."

And I reiterated, "I think I love you too."

And without ever having had a chance to free my arms and wrap them around his neck, we were walking in the direction of his house again. As we walked, we passed by a few small bridges that crossed over the stream and in the direction of his house. He was holding my hand even tighter.

Chapter 8

The summer finally came and he left. Phone calls were made, flowers were sent (he sent me irises), and a letter was written. He had doodled along the borders of the pages. He drew pictures of stars, flowers, vines, smiley faces and sad faces, spiders and Saturn. It read:

Dearest Donna,

i miss you! i miss you sooo much (it's really incredible). i miss you! i miss you! i miss you! i miss you! i miss you! i miss you! i <u>really</u> miss you! i miss you!

Today is Monday, July 6. The front of this page is the "letter" i said i wrote you on Saturday. i was too tired to do anything but doodle. Right now, it's almost 11:00 at night, and i'm gonna go to bed soon. Gee, this letter doesn't make much sense, but it's the thought that counts, right? God, i miss you so much! i hate it here, but i'm determined to make it through. My body aches everywhere. i want more sleep. Well, i'm going to bed now. i'll probably write again before i mail this so i won't say goodbye. By the way, did i tell you how much i miss you?

Now it's Tuesday, and it's 9:00 in the morning. i had to get up at 6:30 today and run up and down stairs for thirty minutes. My legs feel like Jell-O.

i had a dream about you last night. i dreamt that i went to Canada and found you waiting for me. it was a great dream, i woke up smiling for a change.

i miss you, Donna, a lot! i long to see your face, to see you smile. i long to gaze into your sparkling eyes once again. i want to hold you in my arms again, to press your lips against mine. i miss you more than i can say. i want to go home.

Well, i think i'll finally mail this today, on my way to practice in half an hour. Goodbye.

Chris

(He signed his name next to a picture of a bleeding heart.)

Admittedly, upon reflection, this letter is lacking. It lacks depth and form. Above all, it lacks sophistication. But it is significant. It was the first of a series of correspondence that persisted and matured for many years -as did we.

It is written with the same naiveté with which I used to pray for him: that he would find God, or God him, and that he would make a good wrestler too.

At the time, he did not know how to spell my last name. Less is more.

Exploration and discovery are replete with risk.

How often do people appear to have changed more in two months than in ten, simply because there has been some distance between them? What prompts us to look for and expect changes in people just because we haven't seen them? And when do we see people, *really* see them? When do we begin to chew on their words, their thoughts, before we digest them? When do we regurgitate them? When do differences decide to invade similarities?

It happens when conversations and relationships go deeper -as they are destined to do.

Similarly, it has always been fall's unfortunate fate to follow summer's serenity.

Chapter 9

That is when it started... when he returned from camp and Nova Scotia at the end of August.

"You don't really believe that... do you?" he asked more fearfully than hesitantly.

"Yes," I readily and definitively replied.

"But how could you? I mean how do you explain the dinosaurs? How does the Bible explain the dinosaurs?"

"Oh, I don't know. I hadn't thought about it before."

"And you go to Church *every* Sunday?" He said it as though *that* were a sacrilege.

"Yes."

And then there was silence for a while.

"Do you see him when we're... you know?"

"Who?"

"Him!"

"Oh no, of course not." I knew that he was thinking of the crucifix that hung above my bed.

"Phew!"

And, so, everything was O.K. for a while.

It was still a week before school would start and we set out to spend as much time together as possible. We were entering our junior year of high school. Chris came over to my house on Monday afternoon. We sat in the basement. This time, my parents were home.

"Hey, I read the *Fountainhead* over the summer," I told him.

"Oh, yeah? A guy from my bunk was reading it too. It's a good book."

"Yeah, but I'd like to read it again because I think I missed something. I just don't think I understood everything the first time."

"Hey, did you know that book was based upon the work of Frank Lloyd Wright?"

"No, I didn't, but isn't he the same guy you said visited the Preserve?"

But he didn't answer. He was distracted. He was eyeing the fireplace with contempt.

"Is this a fake fireplace?" he asked.

"Yes." I answered.

I had never given it any thought until just that moment, and, apparently, neither did he. I began to blush. I suddenly felt all the shame I was supposed to have felt over the years for having a fake fireplace in my house.

Then, Chris told me he was going to take Creative Writing this fall. I told him that I had decided to take Expository Writing.

"Why?" he demanded.

"Because most everyone else is taking Expository Writing."

"What?! You're taking it just because everyone else is?!"

"Yes. I assume there must be a good reason for it. There must be good reason why most people tend to do one thing or another more than others. I mean it makes sense when you think about it. Most people go to a doctor when they're sick, run from a fire, eat when they're hungry, and all for good reasons. Right?"

"No! The truth is most people don't go to a doctor when they're sick, most people ignore warning signs until it's too late. As for the other points you made, why then do such things as suicide and anorexia exist?"

He sat staring at the fireplace, shaking his head.

Tuesday, we spent the afternoon at the Preserve. Sitting under the trees near the picnic benches and facing Castle Gould, I was wondering just how many of those eighty-eight rooms had fireplaces, suspecting that all of them must be real.

Chris interrupted my thoughts.

"Hey, what about Job? Did you ever read that stuff?"

"Yeah."

"I mean shit! God puts Job through so much shit, and then Job still has faith?! That's a God for you?! No thanks!," he said, lying on his back, crossing one leg over another, in a 'case closed' manner.

"It wasn't God; it was the Devil," I declared.

"Yeah, but God allowed it. Didn't he?" Chris rebutted.

"No, that's where you're mistaken. God doesn't allow evil; He allows free will, and it's up to us to use it wisely. And Job has faith in God in spite of everything he goes through because, after all, we love our families and friends in spite of everything we put each other through. I mean, love would be easy if life were easy. You can answer the question yourself: As a person, do you want people to love you because they have to or because they want to? And don't you want them to love you in spite of the pain you may cause them, and don't they? Don't they love you anyway? God's just like us in a way."

"Oh, yes! We're created in God's image," he murmured, still lying on his back. Then, he sat up and shouted: "No! That's the giveaway! Don't you see? The Bible says we're created in God's image, but we created the Bible! So we couldn't imagine or create anything more than a God created in Man's image!"

Chris festered as I held fast to my faith.

Wednesday, we had plans to go to the movies. Chris rang the doorbell to my house. When I opened the door, he was standing there, but he wasn't looking at me. Instead, he was staring at the red aluminum siding on my house. Then, his index finger and thumb came together and apart against the red aluminum siding so that all three of them made a "flicking" sound.

"Is this aluminum siding?" he asked as though he had come to appraise the house instead of to pick me up for a date.

"Yes," I said, with as much shame as I felt when I admitted to him that we had a fake fireplace in our house.

We were going to see the film, *The Princess Bride*. Chris was so excited to see it. He informed me that it was his all-time favorite book. I was wondering if I'd like it, hoping I'd like it, afraid I wouldn't like it.

The audience's laughter had confirmed for me that the movie was a comical, satirical portrayal of "true love," and so I could laugh confidently in all the right places, knowing I wasn't insulting him. I didn't want to laugh at the movie if he was taking it seriously. But he wasn't. He was laughing too -what a relief! I enjoyed it.

When it was over, Chris said it was "Excellent!" The movie had done justice to his favorite book, excepting that Buttercup could have been more beautiful.

"I'd like to read the book," I said to him on our way home.

"I don't think you'd get it... you'd like it," he told me, once again the appraiser.

Nevertheless, we went home to his house. We climbed the stairs to his bedroom; he took off my clothes, and then his own. It was understood between us that that's how it would always be, that that was the order in which I liked it done, and yet I never had to use any words to tell him this, to tell him what I liked when we were in bed.

On Thursday, at my house, I hospitably offered Chris a drink, a bite to eat. I poured two glasses of water and held one in my hand. Then, I opened the refrigerator door with the other. Chris peered over my shoulder under the guise that he was hungry. But, then, he reached his arm and hand over mine and accosted the white bread.

"How can you eat that stuff? It's nothing but plastic! You can't even digest it!"

Then, I made the grave mistake of opening the cold cut drawer because he espied the American cheese.

"And this too," he said, taking it in his hands. "It's the most unnatural thing for you. It's processed!"

And the next thing I knew, he was shaking a piece of American cheese mercilessly between two fingers. The plastic was rattling. He made it so that it did look like a piece of rubber or something alien. And I almost chimed... chanted... "Yes! Death to the cheese!" And I was thinking this must be how revolutions begin. But mostly, I was bewildered.

We didn't see each other for the Labor Day weekend because I went camping in Montauk with my parents. My brother didn't accompany us because he had already begun his freshman year in college. After years of traveling up and down the east coast to places like Maine, Pennsylvania, Delaware and Virginia, my parents confined our camping excursions to a campground called Hither Hills in Montauk. One tradition that followed us no matter where we camped was the way we fussed, or argued, over where to pitch the tent. Each of us had an opinion, especially my father and brother. Occasionally, the next day, we might arrive at the conclusion that we should have pitched it elsewhere, facing a different direction because of the sun, the wind or our neighbors. For such occasions, or mistakes, my mother repeated the phrase, "shoulda, woulda, coulda," which we all eventually subscribed to and submitted to. But Hither Hills was always a choice destination because it was only a two and a half hour drive from Port Washington and my mother relished the beach, even if her sun-sensitive skin forced her to sit beneath layers of clothes and blankets. The campsites were conveniently situated on the other side of the sand dunes. We could hear and feel the sound of the ocean waves well into the night within our tent and, amazingly, well into the week once we returned home to our house. It took a while for the sensation to wear off.

The Hamptons were already characterized as a place of wealth and exclusivity at this point. Camping presented itself as the only viable option for a family like mine to partake of its burgeoning popularity and appeal. Every morning, we fetched water, which we boiled on a kerosene stove and with which we washed dishes. Every afternoon, we lay on the beach, occasionally taking a walk along the water, appreciating the beauty of the beach, as well as the magnificence and enormity of the newly built houses. In our imaginations, we lived in those houses. My mother often spoke of owning one some day; although, we all knew that such a dream would never come to fruition.

At night, my father fiddled with a kerosene lamp and built a fire. My mother often joked that my father had missed his calling: he should have been a cowboy. For entertainment, we talked, ate marshmallows, played an occasional game of *Trivial Pursuit*, or drove into one of the neighboring Hampton towns to see a movie. At the movie theater, we might run into one or two acquaintances from school with their respective families. In all likelihood, they were staying at an expensive hotel, if not in an extravagant home of their own. But, at the movies, all things appeared equal –never mind that I had taken an open air shower with nothing to conceal my naked body from the eyes of the other waiting women except for a towel that my mom dutifully held up.

I recognized that vacationing in Montauk amounted to a matter of simple pleasures and convenience, but I also realized that it amounted to a matter of inspiration. In other words, it was one of my parents' attempts to keep my brother and I close to the borders of opportunity and aware of possibilities beyond the scope of their own origins and current capabilities. My parents did not go to college; so, attending a SUNY school, as my brother did, was an accomplishment. In the absence of my brother, I had more time to think about the sense of humility, appreciation and promise that my parents gave us, which is why Chris's abutting criticism became more and more unbearable when I returned home and to school. He could never really appreciate the simplicity in which I was raised, in which I lived, nor could he appreciate the good intentions of my parents. No matter how much he professed to love nature, he couldn't really "see the forest for the trees."

Once school began, and after I experienced one day of Expository Writing, I switched into Comparative World Literature. During the first week of classes, I stood at my locker. Chris approached me from the other end of the hall. When he came closer, he asked, "What's in your hands?"

"It's my reading assignment for Comparative World Literature. It's called *The Grand Inquisitor.* It's about a Cardinal who confronts Jesus and tells Him He should never have given Man free will, and that the Church has changed all that by telling people how to behave. He warns Jesus not to interfere with the work of the Church. I guess the Cardinal thinks that Jesus overestimated our goodness and intelligence. It's basically a criticism of the hierarchy of the Catholic Church."

"Sounds like good stuff," he said.

I slammed my locker door in response.

"Ughh!," was the next thing that escaped from his mouth.

"What's the matter?"

"Your fingers look bloody."

I was wearing red nail polish; that was all. I seldom wore nail polish again. We headed down the hall.

Then he said: "Here, this is what I wanted to give you. You should read this."

"What is it?"

"*Tracks*, by Louise Erdrich."

I stopped and took the book in my hands. I looked at the cover and said, "What is she, an Indian?"

"A Native American," he corrected. "You shouldn't call them Indians any more. I mean we shouldn't have called them that in the first place. Anyway, you should read about them. They're *really* spiritual people. They have so much respect for the land and the moon and stuff. I mean, they honor everything under the sun as though it were a deity. Not like us."

That was fuel for my fire. "So, you denounce monotheistic religions, but not polytheistic religions. Is that it? Is that right? How can you do that? Draw lines indiscriminately? Either you think people should believe in a God or gods, or not! And then you don't like nail polish, or make-up or jewelry. You say it's all nothing but self-adornment, but the Indians were into it! Self-adornment is inherent within all cultures! And wasn't it you who said you wanted to get an earring not too long ago?!"

I dropped the book on the floor and walked away, but not before I heard him correct me with a mumble, "They're Native Americans."

It eventually got to the point that we couldn't last anymore. What was the last straw? It might have been *The Bronx Zoo*. My parents and I had taken him with us to see the pandas. It was all too much for him: the peanuts, the cages, and our holding hands throughout it all in a horrific act of consummation of it. Chris just couldn't understand man's necessity to imprison animals, particularly the American people, who were living in "the land of the free and the home of the brave." It was a wonder to me that he had agreed to come at all. I suppose it was O.K. to have pet snakes but Not OK to contain other kinds of animals in a zoo. I was reminded of our previous conversation about the Native Americans and their gods. (I could concede to calling them by their rightful name and I eventually read Erdrich's book with enjoyment.) However, I still felt frustrated.

He said he wanted to talk about it in person. So he said he was coming over.

I took the cross my parents had given me for my ninth grade Confirmation out of its box and I hung it around my neck. I wore it outside my shirt. I did it out of spite. I wanted him to see it. I wanted him to reject it, or accept it -me, that is.

We went for a walk to the park at the end of my street. That's where it ended -at the picnic benches.

Chapter 10

By now, it was the end of October. We drifted into anonymity for the next six months of school -a time when you no longer know each other, but know *of* each other. During that time, I knew that he had had a birthday in January, took his road test in February, had had another girlfriend in April, and finally got the earring he had once told me he had wanted in May. Most of the time, he wore a feather dangling from his ear. Other times, he wore a crystal or a shark's tooth. During our second semester, we shared another class -a math class. From the fourth seat from the front, and in the row closest to the windows, I heard from a voice to which I used to speak.

Sometime in May, I took a walk through Sands Point. From my house, I had traveled as far as the point where Dunes Lane intersects with Cornwall Lane. I was taking the back way from Manorhaven into Sands Point. Just then, Chris appeared on his bicycle. He was coming the other way from Cornwall Lane towards Dunes Lane. He stopped. I stopped. We said hello. It felt funny seeing each other there like that. After all, we hadn't spoken in six months. We could have been taking a walk together, riding our bicycles, clearing our heads, being outdoors, engaging in all the things we both liked to do. That's what I was thinking at the time.

Now, when I think back on that "chance" encounter, I laugh; I laugh at how often happenstance and fate are misinterpreted in life.

Then, one night, early in June, there was a party at Sam's. It was a small party. Sam was a mutual friend of ours. He lived just three houses down from Chris. Their families were good friends. Chris and I, along with three others, sat outside on the front porch. The conversation carried itself in a group of five but then, one by one, the others left.

Chris was sitting on the porch banister, wearing a gray tank and cut-off jeans. It was incredibly hot. He was sweating profusely. Despite the sun and the heat we were having in June, Chris was pale. He didn't believe in sun bathing, just trees and the shade.

I was wearing cut-off jeans and a cropped long-sleeved black cotton T-shirt. I already had a deep, dark, tan. I stood there with my arms crossed in front of me. It was awkward. What does one do with a "moment?" -a moment like this and with his house dangerously close.

"Wow! You look beautiful," he said.

"Thank you," I said and looked towards the door. Sam had just opened it. He took a minute to take us in and then he said, "Donna, come on in, I'll get you a beer. I didn't even know you were out here."

"Yeah, O.K.," I said. Sam held the door open for me. I looked back at Chris, said bye, and went inside.

Later that night, when I was leaving, I found Chris still sitting on the banister. Outside, he had carried on conversations with people who had come and gone during the night. I wanted it to happen too.

"Hey, are you leaving?" he asked.

"Yeah."

We stood opposite one another for a moment.

"Yeah," I said again, reading his mind.

He jumped off of the banister, took my hand, and we walked the three houses to his own.

His house is the color of brick red. The grass is overgrown. A consequence of intent or neglect, I don't know, but as we were walking, I recall that Chris once mentioned he found landscaping offensive. Was he referring to the use of an electric lawnmower? Was he talking about the rich people of Port Washington employing landscapers in feudal fashion? Or was he alluding to people (and corporations) who make animals out of their shrubbery?

It's funny, then, that the kitchen window of Chris's house looks like the window of a greenhouse. From the street, the entire kitchen is visible through the window. Now, let me take you down the steps. Walk straight for about three or four steps. Turn your head to the right.

See the picnic table and the barbecue? Now, up again three or four steps. Open the screen door. There is a wooden shelf next to the door to the garage. There are raincoats, an assortment of shoes and boots, as well as a basket. Turn to your right and open the door to the kitchen. There isn't any bell to ring, but someone will hear you if you knock loudly enough. Whether or not someone lets you in, you feel as though you're letting yourself in. The second door is heavier than the screen door.

Just before you enter the kitchen, there's another door that leads to the basement. That's where his sister sleeps when she comes home from college. That's where the snakes live. You have to duck when you go down the stairs. But we're not going down.

The kitchen is old. I can barely see the cars parked on the street from the window. The floor is the color of brick red. It creeks. The newspapers are on the table. Sometimes, there are shoes on a chair or even on the table. A liberty, I thought. Above the table hangs a framed picture of a whale's fin. A few years later, Chris's family removed the fin and hung a photograph of a ship Laurel sailed on as a cook -the same ship Chris would sail on just a year after Laurel.

To the right of the doorway to the hallway hangs a chalkboard for phone messages. Three wire baskets hang in tiers above the garbage can. That's where the bread

48

goes. The garbage can is off-white. It's the kind that has a pedal that you have to step on to open it.

Step into the hallway. Step up again because the carpet is thick, comfortably thick, and rust colored. You can't go straight for very far -only about two feet. Look directly in front of you. There's a rectangular picture staring at you. It was photographed in three different shots, and not all of the photos have the same amount of light in them. The property is situated on a long strip of beach, but there are lots of trees in it too. I can barely see the houses. There are lots and lots of trees. It's Nova Scotia.

O.K., now go right toward the living room. It's the biggest room in the house. Don't look at the picture on the wall to your left that a friend made for Chris's parents in shades of gray and brown. It scares me. But there's one that makes me laugh. A woman sits with an arched and playful back on a chair while her husband pulls her by her hand. Her other hand hangs over her forehead as though she were about to faint. The woman is saying "Oh, yes!" and the inscription reads: "for Jeff and Dawn." A friend of theirs made that one too -maybe it was the same friend who made the scary picture. I could never have imagined the same picture hanging in my house. Neither modesty nor morality would permit it. Another liberty, I thought. A closet stands between the two pictures.

Then, there's the corner where the Christmas tree is at Christmas time. Next to the Christmas tree spot, sits the stereo. On top of the stereo, sits one of the characters from *Where The Wild Things Are*. At Christmas time, he sits on top of their tree. He's their angel and yet another liberty.

There are lots of windows in the living room. I always wondered just how much you could see of the living room from the street, and I often would look, myself, as I drove by.

They have a fireplace on that side of the room too, but a real one, needless to say. A picture hangs above it with thin streaks of red, yellow and blue on a white backdrop. I guess you could say it's a graphic design. The picture reminds me of a prism.

Now, turn away from the wall with the windows, so that you're facing the third wall. There's another door. Is it the front door? It has all the formality that front doors have, like a cement walkway and doorbell, but it's in an awkward place. It faces a busy street, so there isn't any place to park a car. It isn't a useful entrance by any means, whether or not a part of the couch sits directly in front of it, as it did. I always wanted to take the liberty of walking through that door.

To the right of the door, hangs a yarn-like wall hanging, which his sister may or may not have made. I just don't remember. It looks like a large spool of thread when it doesn't look like a multicolored hourglass.

Make another right. There's the fourth wall. Your eyes will spot some white shelves and trinkets that I, myself, never examined too closely. Somehow, that corner of the room seemed miles away. Then, there's another doorway -minus the actual door- leading into the dining room. Now, your back faces all the windows I just told you about a little while ago. Can you see anything? No? I didn't think that you would. It's usually dark in there. Anyway, there's just a very plain wooden table and a china cabinet. I doubt there's any China in there. We once ate take-out Chinese food off of plastic plates in there.

There are pictures and books lined up between the dining room entrance and the kitchen entrance. I remember some. There's a picture of Laurel taken outdoors holding some purple flowers in front of her face with one hand. The front of her hair is pulled back in a clip. It's a beautiful picture. There's a picture of Chris's parents at a gathering down the street. There's a picture of Ernest Hemingway and his great-grandfather, the inventor. Chris has the same black, puffy eyes that his great-grandfather had. There's a woman holding a harp between her legs in an empty, open, big, brown room. The woman is Chris's grandmother. The picture was taken in Canada. There's a picture of Chris's mother and her sisters in Canada —maybe in the same empty, open, big, brown room. Looks like it. They were always changing: the pictures on top of the books. Ah, the books. I loved the books!

A beige couch, made of cloth, lies in the center of the room and always with a blanket or two thrown on top of it. There are lots of pillows. The seats of the couch are deep enough for two people to lie down side by side if they want to, as Chris and I used to do.

Give me your hand. Come, I'll take you upstairs. Follow me. Exit the living room. Pass the doorway to the kitchen on your left and Nova Scotia on your right. Oops. I forgot all about Laurel's old bedroom. Funny it was, that bedroom -off the kitchen like that. Go ahead, we won't go in, but look inside. See the mattress on the floor, the desk, and the painting she made of a flower. It was a big flower: colored orange and red. It was very beautiful. There are more photographs and a closet inside that bedroom.

The bathroom is adjacent to it. Surprisingly, it had many mirrors. "Look, that's us," he said as he made me look more than once when we passed by it.

The stairs are there too with more thick, comfortable carpet on them. More pictures adorn the wall of the stairs. Chris's father sits in a chair with his feet up on a desk and his hands folded in his lap -his office, no doubt. There's another of Chris's mother with long hair holding little Laurel close to her face. And, of course, there's a photo of little Chris walking barefoot.

The stairs. I went first. Chris followed.

Down the hall is his parents' bedroom. Across from their bedroom is another bathroom. It has a slanted roof. It's modern. Why did they have modern bathrooms? I wanted to know. They didn't fit in with the mattresses on the floor, the old kitchen cabinets and the overgrown grass.

Chris's bedroom was painted green -lime green. The carpeting was a darker shade of green. It didn't go, but it was comfortable -almost as comfortable as the carpeting in the living room and on the stairs. He had a tall bookshelf that held his books and wrestling paraphernalia.

Chris's bedroom led to another room. I walked in and stood in the middle of it. It was their junk room, I guess. It was difficult to tell exactly what its purpose was because you could only obtain access to it by walking through Chris's room first. It always seemed bizarre to me that the house had been designed with only two "official" bedrooms (Chris's and his parents' -Laurel's didn't count since it was off of the kitchen). Apartments may have only two bedrooms, but houses rarely do. But there were more books in this room. There were rows and rows of *National Geographic* magazines. I envied the volume of books they had. It meant that they read. I turned around and faced Chris.

All this time, he had been waiting. He waited while I took everything in as if I were seeing it all for the first time; he was very much aware that the seduction had already begun. The blinds were still open. He seemed never to close them, unless it was a matter of necessity. There was a white light attached to the upper right hand corner of the window. Chris walked to the window, took the wand in his hand and began to close the blinds. Then, he reached his hand to the light and turned it on. Turning on that one light by the window, as he now did, had been a ritual. Other, more inhibited, teenagers would have turned it off at this time.

Below the window, there was a desk. It wasn't an ordinary desk. It was wood and it had once been a door. On one end, the door rested on a filing cabinet, and the other end of it rested on a wooden shelf. His computer sat on top of the desk. Of course, he had a chair to sit in, but again, it was unusual in comparison to the desk. It was one of those modern chairs without any back to it. It's the kind that has a place to pull back your feet. It professed to be a better means of support for the back.

No, their house did not boast of style or uniformity, only warmth, comfort, necessity and a keen sense of knowledge. "They're not pretentious people," my mother often commented with apparent approval.

I turned from the window and looked at the radio next to the bed. Chris was sitting on the bed and had his fingers on the knob. Like Laurel's, the bed was a mere mattress that lay on the floor. Then, Chris moved from one end of the bed to the other so that he sat at the foot of it.

He pointed to the wall and said, "Look. It's my family tree. One of my cousins constructed it this year." Chris pointed to his great-grandfather, the famous inventor. "Hey, did I ever tell you about him?" Chris rhetorically asked me.

Then, he got up off the bed and came toward me. I was thinking of his heritage. He was thinking of me. I was laughing inside thinking about the overgrown grass just below, and that I shouldn't tell him right now that my grandfather had been a landscaper.

Chapter 11

I let myself in the door of my house well past 3:00 A.M. that night. I treaded slowly through the living room so as not to wake my parents; as I did, I took a look around. Like Chris's house, once again, my house seemed new to me too.

I paused at the David, Michelangelo's David. My grandfather's brother, Uncle Johnny, gave a miniature version of it to my mother as a gift when he came over from Italy for a visit in 1963, B.C. B.C., according to my mother, stood for the period of her life before children, which would just about be the most blasphemous thing she's ever said. My mother valued the miniature statue of David above everything else in the house. "If you had been a boy," my mother told me, "your name would have been Michael Angelo" (Angelo, for my grandfather). But, instead, I was a girl, and she named me Donna after my grandfather's sister who wanted to be a nun, and who would have been, except for the fact that she fell sick and the convent wouldn't take her. Instead, she lived out her spinster life wearing nothing but brown in a little Neapolitan village called St. George. My mother said she prayed for us, all of us, every day. I'm not sure whose shoes are harder to fill: Michelangelo's or my Aunt Donna's.

Next to the David, there are pictures of my parents when they were in their teens. I always thought that my mother bore a resemblance to Natalie Wood, and my father was equally good looking. My parents' names are Maria and Tony, just like the lead characters in *West Side Story*, which always pleased me, a literary buff, when I thought about it. My mother has often said to me: "Sometimes, you have a hard time distinguishing between your books and reality."

There are pictures of my grandparents surrounding the pictures of my parents. My mother's parents were Neapolitans. My father's parents were too, but this wasn't a well-known fact in the neighborhood because my father's mother died when he was young; so, he was raised by his Sicilian stepmother. You can bet that if an Italian had written *Cinderella*, she would have had a Sicilian stepmother. You can also bet that, before my mother's father found out that my father's real mother had been Neapolitan, he didn't completely approve of the match. Italians are parochial people.

There are also a couple of photos of my brother and me. One is from the early seventies; it is a picture of us as the ring bearer and flower girl in my godmother's wedding. That day, my brother wore a white shirt with pink-fringed ruffles alongside the buttons underneath his tuxedo. I wore a pink colonial style dress, equipped with a built-in-hoop, that my mother made for me. The dress was trimmed with the same pink fringe that my brother wore on his shirt. Although I'm not wearing it in the picture, my mother also made me a matching bonnet. At the time, my brother was five, and I was three.

When my brother was nineteen, and I was seventeen, we took a similar photograph. My brother wore a tuxedo and, for a second time, I wore the pink Sweet Sixteen dress my mother had made for me. We were going to a party celebrating our parents' twenty-fifth wedding anniversary. I happen to think that the two pictures, because of the color of our clothing in each, stand in perfect juxtaposition to one another.

We have a cream-colored leather couch in our living room. When we first got it, Chris ran his hand over it, asked my mother if it was real leather, and frowned when she said, "Yes". That was still one more thing that did not pass muster, in his opinion. At the time, I wanted to say: "Your sister's a vegetarian, not you! So what's the big deal?" I also wanted to know why he never bothered to acknowledge the real fireplace we now had in our living room -or the fact that my father had built it all by himself.

Upon my mother's insistence, we have a secretary in our living room. On the top shelf of the secretary, from left to right, are the following books: McGraw Hill's *Life of Christ*, Scribner's *Ernest Hemingway-A Life Story*, *National Geographic's Our Country's Presidents*, *Gone With The Wind*, Hyman's *The Complete Home Medical*

Encyclopedia, Popular Mechanic's *Do-It Yourself Encyclopedia Volume 3,* William Shakespeare - *The Collection of Biography and Autobiography, Webster's New World Dictionary,* Globe Book Company's *Better English Through Practice,* and a 1928 edition of *David Copperfield.*

On the second shelf of the secretary, there is a display of five cups and saucers, a sampling of a larger collection of eclectic cups and saucers my mother has collected over the years, and of which I am very fond. My mother is known for her hosting skills. She is known for making her own felt napkin holders: red flowers with green leaves for Christmas and pink flowers with green leaves for Easter.

There are more books on the third shelf: *The Readers Digest Collection of Best Loved Books for Young Readers* (Volumes 1-12), which is a composite of the classics in bindings representing every color of the rainbow -and then some. When I was younger, my mother gave me Volume 6, *Little Women,* to read. I loved it. I hear that a mother's license is revoked if she does not hand her daughter Louisa May Alcott's novel by the time she leaves her teens. There is also a medal, blessed by the Pope, on that same shelf.

On the other side of the fireplace, nearing the dining room, there is a portable bar. In it, my father keeps decks of playing cards for holidays when my relatives want to play poker. On top of the bar, my mother placed the anniversary clock that my brother and I gave our parents for their twenty-fifth anniversary. Some years later, the bar would collect high school graduation photos and off-to-college photos of my brother and me. In the college photos, my brother and I are standing beneath billboard-size signs with our colleges' names in big letters on them because my mother made us. I thought we looked like a couple of ignoramuses, announcing to the world just how big a deal it was for us to be going to college. But anytime I would come close to saying this or suggesting we get rid of those photos, my mother would get angry. So, after a while, I just left it alone.

There is another clock above the bar. It's an old, antique clock that my mother's brother picked up in Germany while he was in the service. My mother's brother was a schizophrenic who compounded his problems with drug abuse. He died of pneumonia when I was in the fifth grade. I realized about ten years later that he must have died from AIDS, and my mother confirmed my suspicions when I asked her. The clock was never known to work until, one night, when my brother decided to take it down and clean it. It turns out, quite by coincidence, that my brother took it down the same night that my uncle ended up dying. As my brother was cleaning it, it started to chime, and it's been working ever since. The "coincidence" still gives my mother and me the chills; so, now that it does work, we keep it turned off. Something of the supernatural or cosmic presided in our house and far less of the scientific, as it did in Chris's. The closest his family came to the issue was the textbooks his father still had from his collegiate studies on schizophrenia.

In the dining room, a picture of Jesus and his apostles seated at The Last Supper hangs on the wall, as it does in most Italian homes. A cross hangs in every bedroom of our house too. The one hanging in my brother's room is a little different, though. It opens up, and inside, there are candles wrapped in plastic and there is a vial of oil. On the inside of the cross, where Jesus' hands would be, there are two holes in which to stand the candles. It used to be more common for people to die and receive the final sacrament, The Anointing of the Sick, in their homes, and that is the reason for having a cross like this one in the home.

"Through this holy anointing, may the Lord in his mercy and love help you with the grace of the Holy Spirit. May the Lord who frees you from sin save you and raise you up," says the priest as he absolves people with the sprinkling of holy oil on various parts of their body, places which have changed over time: the back of the neck, throat, loins, forehead, upturned hands, and the ailing part of the body. It was thought that the senses should be anointed with oil because it is the senses that fall prey to sin. My mother, a Eucharist minister, told me all of this.

My mother made the lace curtains that hang in the living room and dining room windows. My father tore down the wall separating the dining room and living room, laid tile floors, wallpapered, paneled, painted, and did much more over the years.

We all share the same bathroom. It's a yellow and brown bathroom. Our magazine rack features the monthly *Knights of Columbus* magazine, the *U.S. Catholic, People, The Port Washington News* and *The Port Washington Sentinel.*

My parents' bedroom is very plain. There are two closets, one chair in between them, two end tables, two dressers, one mirror, one bed, and a picture of birds in flight above it, looking something like souls blessed with the Holy Ghost ascending into Heaven. My parents' wedding picture and the Bible are positioned in opposite corners of one of the dressers.

I finally crawled into bed, which was covered with a white eyelet comforter at the time. At one time, I had had a pink and white-checkered comforter my mother had made for me. When I was seven years old, my parents allowed me the liberty of decorating my own room. I chose large pink and white-checkered flowered wallpaper to go with the comforter. The wallpaper was later replaced with forest green paint, which was also at my request.

As I closed my eyes, I thought of how little my house, my history, resembled Chris's.

Chapter 12

The very next day, the phone rang.

"Hello?"

"Donna? Hey, how about I pick you up?" It was around 7:00 p.m.

"O.K."

The Community Synagogue is located on Sands Point Road. There were no parties to go to that night. Chris drove us around for a while and then finally decided on the Synagogue as our destination. A very high brick wall surrounds the premises. We parked the car and chose a tree close to the entrance and on the inside of the wall.

"So, how did this happen?" he began. "How does this happen? We used to get along fine. It's not that I don't miss you sometimes. It's just that we're so different. I mean you're a Catholic and I'm just not. I don't know why we didn't see it right away. We're too different." Then, Chris looked away and said, "Donna, you know I'm going to be leaving for the summer again don't you? I'm going to wrestling camp again and then to Canada, as usual."

"Yeah, I know."

"And you know that when I'm gone..."

"No, yeah, I know," I said. I could sense what was coming. This goodbye wasn't going to be like last year's goodbye when he had sacrificed a tournament for me and said he loved me.

"I just don't want you to think..."

"No. I know." Stop, I thought. Do you have to say it? Don't say it. Let me pretend. If you say it, then I can't pretend it could work... me being Catholic and you being an atheist.

Nevertheless, the night before Chris was leaving, we found ourselves at his house again. We had spent a lot of time together during the last two weeks. We couldn't seem to stay away from one another in spite of his speech at the synagogue.

But it wasn't like I remembered it a year ago. A year ago, it was polite. It was exploratory. I remembered the way he had politely folded my clothes the day he stayed home from wrestling camp to be with me. It was as though he were saying: "Hi, how are you?" Would you like to sit down? What would you like to drink?" But, this was lust. This was urgency. He took his hand and wiped my stomach, showed it to me, to my face, and said:

"Don't you feel that?! Don't you feel that heat?!"

My stomach was a pool of sweat.

"Donna...?"

"No."

"But I care for you more than any other guy..."

"Bullshit, and he thought the fake fireplace and aluminum siding were cheesy!" I thought to myself. "No," was what I answered aloud.

Chapter 13

I went away too that summer. My parents sent me to stay with a family in France. This occasion arose because a schoolteacher, Michel, had come to the U.S. with his students for three weeks during the spring. We housed Michel. In turn, he invited me to visit his family in France for three weeks in July. I couldn't help but think that it was romantic, like something out of an Edith Wharton or a Jane Austin novel.

The same day that my plane flew into Lyon, we left in a car for southern France. We were headed for a small village by the name of St. Andéol de Berg, just near a larger town called Ville Neuf de Berg. Michel's mother had grown up in that village, in the same house to which we were headed. The family now used it as a vacation home in the summers.

The house was at the end of the street. St. Andéol really only had one street. The house had three bedrooms and one common room, a very spacious kitchen. I had my own bedroom during the week, but on the weekends, Michel's wife, Véronique, shared it with me. Véronique only came down for the weekends because she had to work at a hospital in Lyon during the week. She was a nurse. Michel, his brother, Philippe, and Michel's two children, Élisabeth and Frédéric, shared one of the other two bedrooms. Michel's parents occupied the third bedroom. I felt guilty for having a whole bedroom practically to myself, but they insisted that it be that way.

I enjoyed our dinners together. They were ceremonious; everyone had their own cloth napkin and napkin holder, with their name on it, to be used everyday. Dinners reminded me of my own family because, in France, we ate in the late afternoon -just as my family did on Sundays at home. We didn't all eat breakfast together, and that's because everyone was allowed to rise at their leisure, especially me. The first morning I woke up, Michel's mother gave me a basin of water, one towel, and two washcloths. I used one washcloth for my face and the other for my body, and was very careful not to confuse the two during my stay. That's how I "showered" everyday. They had an outdoor toilet, presumably habited by scorpions, though I, myself, never saw one.

Michel, Philippe, and their father were all fond of opera music, which they played every morning. When I would wake up in the mornings, I'd open my bedroom window, which faced the yard, and see all three of them sitting in chairs, or even lying on the wall of stone that surrounded the yard. I took great pleasure in their serenity. That was the mornings.

In the afternoons, we went to the swimming pool in Ville Neuf de Berg. I liked the drive there because Michel and Philippe were forced to honk the horn every time we went around a bend to make sure that we didn't run into a car coming from the other direction. A Belgian family camped near Ville Neuf de Berg and came to the pool everyday too. The two families were friends and so I spent a lot of time with them too. Occasionally, we all went to a café in the evenings, where I drank some wine too. Uninhibited, I spoke French with greater ease under the influence of the wine.

I spent the time between our rendez-vous, meals, and swimming, doing some reading. One day, I sat in the yard reading Sartre's *Les Jeux Sont Faits*. When Philippe saw me reading it, he gave me Sartre's *Existentialism and Human Emotions* to read too. This was my first introduction to Sartre and existentialism; both fascinated me. I learned that existentialists believe in taking responsibility for their actions; however, they do not believe in lamenting them. Existentialists believe in freedom, choices, and opportunities. They do not believe in regrets, or obsessing over what they could have or should have done. I was reminded of my mother saying, "shoulda, woulda, coulda," and smiled thinking that its meaning bore some resemblance to existentialism. Anyway, in a small way, being an existentialist is like "not crying over spilt milk." But seriously, it made sense to me. Not only is regret a moot point, but it's a waste of energy. Isn't that why people say, "let bygones be bygones," because there's simply nothing you can do to affect or change the past?

I got to thinking: All we ever do at any one point in time is make the best of all possible decisions with the best knowledge that experience and time afford us. Voltaire teaches us that in *Candide*-well, sort of. Well, anyway, it made sense to me. It was practical. It was sensible. I embraced it.

So, existentialists do not believe in regret; nor do they believe in God. But that's the funny thing about philosophies and religions: We adopt them in some way, shape or form, though rarely in their entirety.

It was then that I arrived at the definitive conclusion that I would never, could never, be sorry for anything I did.

One day, we went kayaking with the Belgium family in Ardèche. The scenery was beautiful. I remember three landmarks along Les Gorges. At the starting point, we had passed under an arc simply called Le Point D'Arc (the point of the arc). Then, there had been a bridge overhead called Le Point du Diable (the point of the devil). Finally, there was a formation way up high on the rocks, which was likewise made of rocks, called La Cathédrale because of its resemblance to a Cathedral.

We weren't alone. There were many other people kayaking too. At first, there were lots of topless women, but that had ceased to faze me by now.

Then, there were naked people... lots and lots of naked people. There were hoards of naked people -naked families, meaning husbands, wives, mothers, fathers, and children. They weren't in the kayaks. They were off to the side; they were sunbathing on the rocks. I couldn't see beyond the naked people. I couldn't believe it: mothers and fathers naked with their children!

"Michel," I said, "are those people French?"

"No, not at all. They are mostly German. They are tourists. They are on vacation like you... like us... but they are naked."

"I know. I can see that. I can't believe it. I've never seen anything like it. It's not like a nude beach either. It's different. These are families."

"Yes."

"I feel like I'm in the Garden of Eden -had Adam and Eve not eaten the apple, of course. This is so strange. They're comfortable -almost too comfortable. They make me feel strange." The nakedness, the strangeness... called to mind Chris and his eccentricities.

Chapter 14

I tried to call Chris a day or two after I got home from France.

"Hello?"

"Hi, Mr._____?" Chris's parents always wanted me to call them by their first names, but I couldn't do that. "It's Donna. Is Chris home?"

"No, he's still in Canada. Dawn came home not too long ago but Chris decided to stay a little longer. He's going to catch a ride with his cousins. He wants to get in some more partying before he comes home, especially now that he has the house all to himself. It's hard to drag him away from there." Partying? That was a word neither of my parents would have used with any tone of approval. But, then, I didn't discuss smoking pot with them either, like Chris did with his parents.

"Oh, O.K.," I managed to say, but I wasn't able to say goodbye or hang up.

After a pause, his father said, "I could give you the phone number in Canada. You could call him there if you want," he offered.

"O.K. Thanks."

Later, that same night, I called him.

"Hello?"

"Chris?"

"No. Hold on a sec."

"Hello?"

"Chris?"

"Yeah?"

"It's Donna."

"Hey, what's up?"

"Nothing. I just got back from France."

"Hey, how was it?"

"Good. Really good."

"Excellent!"

"How about your summer?"

"Oh, it's been a blast. We're having such a good time. Right now, I'm throwing a party in my house. We've got all these people here. It's excellent."

"Oh, cool," I said. I could here the music and voices in the background.

"So, what's up?" he asked.

"Remember the last night we spent together before you left?"

"Yeah?"

"Well, I changed my mind."

"Oh. Ohhh...."

"So, when will you be coming home?"

"I'll be coming home in about a week."

"O.K. Well, I'll see you when you get back."

"Yeah, O.K. Bye. Uh, goodnight."

"Goodnight."

I went to bed with naked tourists and existentialism on my mind that night. Is it possible that romanticism can disguise itself in such a way?

Set me on an Ocean Wind, Set me on a Course of Sin.

About a week later, the phone rang.

"Donna?"

"Chris? You're back?"

"Yeah, listen, I'm going out to dinner with my family... my sister is here... but she's going back to college tomorrow." His sister was beginning her junior year and she was studying marine biology.

"But, listen, there's a party on Old House Lane. You going?"

"Yeah, I heard about it too."

"Meet you there?"

"OK." Before I could ask him what time he thought dinner would end, he was gone, but he left me wondering about more than what time he'd get there. More importantly, I was wondering if this would be it. I hung up the phone and immediately made arrangements with my friends to go to the party. You might think I obsessed over what to wear, but I didn't. I threw on a pair of jean shorts and a black T-shirt. I knew that the party was at a house on the beach. Usually, I dressed up more. I certainly dressed up more than Chris; it was never the other way around.

I decided to wear my hair curly as I always did in the summer. I put some gel in it and let it dry by itself. I put on black eyeliner, nothing more. As a habit, I didn't wear a lot of makeup in high school. It wasn't that I wasn't allowed. I've always blushed easily so I had good color, whether or not it was summer or winter. I've never permed or colored my hair either. I was what you would call "natural." Despite our other differences of opinion, I always figured Chris liked that about me: that (except for nail polish) I chose to go natural, rather than made-up. Intuitively, I knew he wouldn't like it any other way and, coincidentally, that's the way it was. It all sounds so positive, but now I sometimes think upon it as a prejudice we both shared against people who wanted or had to make cosmetic changes.

From the side of the pool, I spotted him at the kegs in white shorts and a green shirt, whose color I hated because it was lime-green. I thought he knew that. He saw me too and motioned me to come his way. In the meantime, he'd gotten a beer for me.

"Hey," he said with a big smile and a lot of enthusiasm. He had a light tan -probably from windsurfing.

"Hi."

"Have you been down to the beach yet?" he asked.

"No."

"Let's go."

We walked away from the lights that surrounded the pool into the darkness of the yard. We came to a gate that separated the yard from the beach, but it was locked. Chris put down his beer. Then, he took mine from my hand and put it down on the ground next to his. He helped me over the fence, passed me the beers, then, he mounted it himself. Once on the other side, we started walking and talking.

"Did you know that the women in Europe go topless on the beaches?" I asked him. I was trying to be provocative in the same way he had been when he asked about the show *Hair*.

"Yeah, doesn't everybody know that?"

"Yeah, but what's the most naked people you've ever seen at once?"

"What? Where? What are you talking about?"

"Well, I saw hundreds of naked people when I was in France."

"Oh yeah? Where?"

"While I was kayaking. They were strewn along the banks of the river. And there was a plethora of fathers and mothers with their children. Don't you think that's incredible? Would you do that with your family?"

"Hell, yeah, but it's not a new concept... it sounds like a commune and we had them all over the place in the sixties." He spoke of the sixties as if he had lived during that era.

Anyway, like I said, I was trying to be provocative, but felt that I was failing miserably until Chris suggested we do the same thing.

"Here?" I asked.

"Yeah. Why not? Have you seen a soul on the beach since we've been here? I haven't."

When I didn't answer, he said, "OK forget it."

We walked a little farther in silence. That wasn't what I wanted either, so I stopped and said, "OK, let's do it."

"You sure?"

"Yeah, but you go first."

So, he took his shirt off and looked at me as if it were my turn. So, I did the same.

Then, he waited for something.

"What?" I asked.

"Your bra too or we can't move on to the shorts."

Then, he took off his shorts and underwear at once.

I looked around nervously. "I don't think I can." I said.

"There's nothing to it. I'll show you."

Then, he walked closer to me. He put his fingers on the button of my shorts and his lips on my mouth.

"Here?" I asked.

"Hmm?"

"Here? Are we going to do it here?"

"Do you want to?"

"Well, I don't know. We don't have a blanket or anything."

"That's OK, we have our discarded clothes we could lie on."

"And what about...?" But I couldn't bring myself to say it. I thought I'd wait for him to say it, but he didn't. He just took off my shorts.

"Wait. We'd have to use something. Do you have anything?"

"No... I've just pulled out before."

Pulled out before? I had heard him, and understood him. It hurt me. This had never come up before; I just assumed he was a virgin too.

"No, I said, that's not enough. Let's just go."

School resumed and so did we. For a while, we didn't speak of what we almost did, but the prospect still lay there, day after day, night after night. I put him to the romantic test, reminding myself of his curiosity for nature, his surge of emotions, his love for the iris and his desire to be original, like no one else. I imagined that he would someday do great things. I conjured up a dream of my own for him: I imagined that he would write a book, and that I would look back with a desire to have known him. I put myself to the existential test more than once too, asking myself about the potential for misgivings. I finally concluded that I'd have no regrets, and since someone I greatly admire once told me, "A lady never tells," I will leave it to your own imagination.

My mother followed me into my room. I had just told her in the car, while we were out shopping on a Saturday afternoon. I had decided I would go on the pill, and I was afraid she'd find out by accident. She sat there on my bed. This was definitely not a scene out of an Edith Wharton or a Jane Austen novel, but it was intense.

With time, of conversations -even the most heated arguments and sentimental encounters -only fragments survive the whole.

She said, "You want me to approve, that's why you're telling me, but I won't approve because I don't agree."

"No, I don't want you to approve. That's not true. I just want to make you understand and accept it."

"No, you want me to approve. You want me to approve so your conscience will be at ease. "

"No, you see, you don't understand... my conscience is already at ease -that's the part you don't understand. Perhaps it would be easier on you if you would accept that. I'm not sorry for what I've done." I was tempted to ask her if she had ever read any existential philosophy, but I refrained.

Instead, I said, "Maybe it would have been better if I hadn't told you." Then, she wouldn't have to bear the weight of knowing, I thought.

"I think maybe it would have been better if I didn't know," she said to conclude the discussion.

Chapter 15

We were invited to a Halloween party in October. I drove my car over to his house, since the party was within walking distance from it. I let myself in the screen door. As I walked into the kitchen, I heard his footsteps descending rapidly on the stairs. Then, he walked into the kitchen. He had an open beer in his hand.

"You're just in time," he said. "Can you zip me up?" He was going as a skeleton.

"Thanks. Want a beer?" he asked, moving toward the refrigerator. Then, as he turned from the refrigerator and handed me the bottle, he took notice of my costume for the first time.

"Cleopatra? A virgin might have been more ingenious."

"Very funny," I said. "Where are your parents?"

"Movie."

As I was drinking, I blurted out, "You know you can't necessarily use science to renounce religion." I had been musing over that thought while I had been getting dressed at home and couldn't wait to spring my insights on him.

"And why is that?" he asked as though this thought was an appropriate segue for us and as he took another beer from the refrigerator for himself.

"Because science is based upon hypotheses that have been proven on earth; whereas, religion is based upon hypotheses that have yet to be proven in Heaven. You cannot speak of them with respect to one another; they are irrespective of one another. They are independent of one another, so to speak, because they exist on different planes. Hence, science cannot be used to renounce religion." Resolutely, I took a chug of my beer.

"O.K., you've got a point."

"And there's still this soul thing anyway," I said.

"What do you mean?"

"Well, I still don't believe that our souls die. I can't believe that my soul dies with my body. I feel too much energy, much too alive, for my soul to die."

"Wait 'till you're old. See how much energy you'll feel then," he said.

"No, I'm serious. Don't you feel the same way? Like you just can't die? Don't you?"

"Nope. Hey Donna, have you ever been to a funeral?"

"Yes. Smartass."

"'Cause you know, we could skip the party and take a stroll through the cemetery this evening if you'd like. Death is inevitable, if not imminent." Then, he raised his beer and said: "O, that this too, too solid flesh would melt," from *Hamlet*. He took a moment to laugh and then he said, "Hey, you could have been an angel tonight. Had you thought of that?"

"So, you don't agree with me about the soul, huh?"

"Nope."

Chapter 16

November came. Like everyone else, we went out the night before Thanksgiving since there wasn't any school the next day. We ended up at the local shopping center with about thirty or more other kids from school, including many of our friends, which is where people went when not too much was going on, or after a party had just been broken up by the police.

It looked like a fight was about to break out. Five senior guys were closing in on one sophomore. Chris was close by, watching this happen, and, being a pacifist, he intervened: He'd told them to leave the guy alone. Then, he murmured something under his breath that I wasn't close enough to hear. But that was it. I always knew that that murmuring he did would eventually amount to no-good. The five guys pounced on Chris. They were beating him up, and now everyone was watching, including our friends. I was astonished to see that only one of them tried to help him, in spite of the fact that I yelled out, "Help him!" But they were scared.

When it was over, Chris turned to walk home. I followed him. We walked in silence. Nearing Baxter Pond, we met up with them again, those five guys. One of them, a guy named Mike, tapped Chris on the shoulder from behind. Chris turned around, and then I did too.

This guy, Mike, said he wanted to shake Chris's hand -call it a "truce." Chris told him to forget it. In response, Mike spit in his face and hit him in the jaw before walking away. He had cracked one of Chris's teeth. As we continued to walk, Chris kept saying: "Can you believe it? He beat me up and then he actually wanted to shake my hand." When we got to his house, we went up to his room, and I held him, while he kept saying: "They didn't do a thing. All my friends were there and they didn't do a thing." I don't think either one of us knew which was worse: what Mike had done or what his friends hadn't done. This time, I had to admit that he had had a legitimate gripe.

The day after Thanksgiving, Chris and I visited the Preserve. We wandered around the grounds of the castle and then toward the picnic benches. As we walked, we passed the American flag. I noticed that Chris was staring malevolently at it.

"Tell me something," he said, "why isn't it always at half mast? Somebody's always dying aren't they? It's not as if one life is more important than another."

In the aftermath of that accusation, we took refuge under a tree. It was unusually warm, so, before we lay down, we each took off our jackets, rolled them up, and placed them under our heads like headstones.

Then, I said, "I think trees resemble our quest for Truth because their branches resemble fingers -fingers

85

that are pointing to the Heavens as if to show us that that's where Truth resides."

"Pointing?... Or are they just reaching?... reaching for the Truth... stretching the truth?" he replied.

"Well, Chris, why shouldn't we expect to find Truth in the Heavens, in God? After all, although Truth isn't intelligible, it must be the most intelligent of entities, and maybe that's why we should believe Truth is God because, given its intelligence and power, it would have to be a god. And maybe the reason we should believe in God is because we believe in Truth."

"But what if I renounce the Truth? What if I renounce the possibility of ever knowing the Truth? Can't I still renounce God then too?"

"No. Not unless you're willing to renounce hope as well. Are you? Then, I recited from the Bible and from memory: 'For, in hope we are saved. Now hope that sees for itself is not hope. For who hopes for what one sees? But if we hope for what we do not see, we wait with endurance.'"

"What's that?"

"The Bible -*Letters to The Romans*," I said.

"That reminds me," he said. "I remember when I first heard the story of Adam and Eve and the Garden of Eden. I was little. I heard it from a friend of the family. But, the way I heard it, it was just a story, like folklore, and I think that the difference between believers and nonbelievers is just like smokers and second-hand smokers: Directly or indirectly, we're all affected."

Chapter 17

For Christmas, my mother made me a black wool cape with a hood and one button at the base of the neck. During the first week of January, I showed up at Chris's house wearing the cape.

"Wow," he said.

I was also wearing a cross around my neck. His eyes fell on the cross as I took the cape off and his face fell as well.

"Don't be sore," I said. I took the cape and threw it on his shoulders.

"What are you doing?"

"Look in my pockets," I told him.

He did. "Garlic?" he asked.

"Yes. When we go upstairs, I'm going to rub it all over your chest."

"Why?"

"Because you're the one they warned me about all my life... In the Scriptures, in my house... and I believe this is the way to destroy you. Isn't it?"

"If I were a vampire, yes, but hasn't anyone ever told you that they don't exist either?"

And then in one fell swoop, Chris took me upstairs with the cape on *his* back. My concern the next day was concealing the love bites on my neck from my mother's eyes.

Chapter 18

"O.K. Donna, I've asked you this before, but how can you be so sure? How can you be so sure they didn't make it all up?"

"Make what up?"

"The Bible. I mean you read. You understand what the imagination can do -what it can create. Lots of books convey messages in morality. Hell, that's what children's books are almost always about -lessons in morality. Surely, you can see that, intellectually, the Bible may just be a good book. Yeah, a damn good book, and someone stumbled upon it somewhere."

"You know," I told him, "sometimes I wonder what it would be like if we had children someday."

"Yeah?"

"Yeah. And I picture that it's their bedtime and we're saying goodnight to them, but not at the same time. I'll go in first, say a prayer with them and tuck them in like my mother used to do with my brother and me. And then I see you going in after me. And they'll make reference to the Bible, to something I just told them, and you'll say: 'Don't listen to her.' And they'll protest; they'll say, 'But mommy said...' And you'll say: 'Don't listen to what your mother tells you. That's not how it goes.' And there's something both pitiful and funny about it all."

At the end of the same month, January, Chris made his announcement in a burger place: "Hey, I got into Michigan everyone."

It was more like an aside, an incidental, than an announcement. He'd said it between bites of his burger. It was a safety school for him. It was an accomplishment that he would later use as testimony to his mediocrity. Basically, he didn't much care.

Michigan had been my first choice, but I had already been rejected. I got up and went to the bathroom. Getting into Michigan would have given me validation; it would have answered all my prayers. I resented his flippancy. I thought I was going to throw up.

We shared the same English class our spring semester senior year. Again, Chris would sit in the fourth or fifth seat, and in the row closest to the windows. English was the first class of the day. He used to waltz in late, if at all. His attendance was terrible, probably because he had just been admitted into college. He would come through the door, walk behind the teacher's desk, walk down the row next to the windows, and, as he did, open one, two or three of them -the windows.

We were all more or less friends in the class. We all knew each other pretty well. Still, this is what would happen:

"Oh man, Chris is gonna come in and open all the windows."

"Yeah."

"Yeah."

There would be a series of grunts and murmurs.

So, I said, "If you guys don't want him to open the windows, tell him." I was still angry with him for getting into Michigan and making light of it. I wanted to punish him. There were just more grunts and murmurs. When he walked in, Chris did exactly as they'd said he would, exactly as he had been doing for a semester, but they did nothing, said nothing. It's not that they were scared of Chris. It wasn't that at all. But what the hell was it then... other than an imposition on his part?

Maybe it had less to do with fear, and more to do with stage presence. After all, he often walked around school barefoot, and he once wore a skirt to class. Well, it wasn't really a skirt, but some blanket or something or other that his sister brought home for him from Kenya. Anyhow, he wore it like a skirt. And, then, there was that hat he wore for a while -that leather hat. It made him look like Indiana Jones. Incidentally, I could never figure out why the leather hat was O.K., but the leather couch was not O.K. And, then, he couldn't just wear an earring. He had to wear a shark's tooth or a long purple crystal. Yeah, he got a kick out of himself, and everyone else seemed to,

too. His eccentricities became an expectation and a form
of entertainment.

Chapter 19

It was February, a school night. The phone rang.

"Hello," I answered.

"Hey, Donna..."

"Oh, hi, Chris."

"Hi."

"What's up?"

"I don't know. I've been doing some thinking, some writing. Can I come over?"

"Yeah, sure."

He came with a knapsack. He reached his hand in and out of it. He gave me this, his first written "monologue:"

hey nay bay bore banana bandana breakfast fast eat break broke poor sorry badshape condition codeblue bluejeans genesplicing idon't ispy hy high hi sty messy room boom soon monsoon pantaloon platoon how brown cow foma fee fi fo fum blood vampire i've got a date with a vampiregirl tonight fire inferno dante dainty ain't he why cain't we paint thee take three penicillin panacea potion pad house home gnome gnew knew news pews pee-u u-stink think pink the panther inspector inspect her no sir justaddwater and stir spill don'tcryoverspiltmilk

silk satin leatherlace ace mace dogfood foodforthought
caught sought distraught fought fight mightmakesright
by right of might intothenight outofsight outofmind what
you don't know won't hurt you cencorshipworks and out
they did spew filth garbage garbonzo beanz i wana laka
caca doo-doo poo-poo shit dung elephantdung
dungbeetles are edible dung-foo kung-foo tae kwan do i
won't go hell no justsayno drugs don't show
youreapwhatyousow sow pig eatsome stew potato
potato tomato tomatohead all is said all are sad some are
mad few are glad this is bad what who hoo ha haha ho
ho merry christmas and a happy new year reindeer wish
you were here how do you feel please kneel heel cold steel
sword swoosh hurrah yippee oh you shouldn't have
where's my staff stave in his skull cave crack oops
whoops let's play some hoops tie the noose i wish she was
loose he looks like a goose or perhaps a moose what the
fuck my car is stuck struck by lightning isn't it exciting
my mind is a dry thing her mind is shallow she is callow
hard to swallow nightingale sparrow hawk fox fox and
the hound foxy lady jack in the box he's got chicken pox i
wear wool sox the clock tick-tocks i go for long walks i
know a dog that talks a god that balks and people who
sputter who stutter my grandma's red sweater i just got
a letter i don't know better life can be bitter the little boy
bit her she was his babysitter got no more wit in her so
won't you excuse me sir try to deter everything is a blur-

blue blabbering blob blubber butt but and more buts-
that's no excuse-because you smell like refuse refuse to go
to the dance with him prance with him in one week i
became slim on this new eezy-off liquid diet isn't that nice
i don't like mice although cats can stay you don't say he
went thatta-way o-kay a horse's neigh...

just stay sober and you'll seem nobler i got a snow
blower it doesn't work the boss is a jerk i feel somewhat
irked i knew a guy named herc if he wore a skirt i would
feel hurt keep your speech nice and curt curtsy cutesy
apple-pie bake me a cake and stick it in your eye cross
your heart and hope to die the big guy in the sky perhaps
you'll sigh into the night or maybe the nile as long as you
wear a smile and stay away from the human race
especially if you're a crocodile who lives in the nile it's the
latest style meet my friend kyle he fell in a pile of shit
suffered a direct hit my sister can't knit she calls me a
twit that dim wit throw him into the bottomless pit and
there i sit does she have zits acne hack me hackneyed
black need a sturdy steed a magic seed that grew into a
stalk that jack climbed to fight the giant rubber bands
are pliant appliances break down planned obsolescence
obsolete isn't that neat a mighty feat he's got two left feet
but he doesn't eat meat his trousers have a pleat the little
lamb begins to bleat so long as i don't flunk i sleep in a
bunk i listen to funk i had a dog who stunk after playing
with a skunk plunk plink think drink sink pink fink the

*king is a stink i write with purple ink i hope my clothes
don't shrink rich bitches wear mink dead animals don't
slink in a wink of an eye i threw through and through
thorough henry james a soldier maims little babies catch
rabies from bats and small gnats buzzing in infinity
barking to a wall barking up the wrong tree crushed in
the mall he was mauled or did he fall perhaps a farewell
fare-thee-well but don't forget to pay the fare taxes axes
on the people's throat who don't own boats and belong to
country clubs hang out with shallow bubs to drink a few
isn't that kind i hope you can find your soul for i am a
mender of souls filet of sole a soul man who got hit with a
frying pan called life which is full of strife and bad guys
with rifles where I can buy food in a plastic bag
processed by the hag of society ruled by the bottom line
the profit motive he had a motive for murder i didn't
want to hurt her but the wench had to be exterminated
totally wasted like a turkey that's been basted is one's
mind when it's tasted the transitory realities of
nonexistent enlightenment brought on by substance or
some other form of entertainment designed to lengthen
one's consciousness to the point of obnoxiousness tv has
carried it way too far we pray it won't mar the body or
soul of a being or a bean it all follows the rhyme scheme
of scheming rhyme and at last we arrive at the scene of
the crime with words and wars we work to fix the error
with preconceived notions of right and wrong we went*

our way man's way through the world of time and space
as if in some apocalyptic race to reach the ultimate goal
the final end of eternal wealth and health rejuvenated as
all our lusts are sated and man's fate debated by those
who care not uncaring unflinching the bullfinch is
flinching and warbler is a'warbling while man in his
worthless twilight explodes in an orgy of power and
force destruction's unleashed as an unbridled horse who
goes neigh...

the earth shatters beneath man's saber and we all take
the novocaine as little babies die playing in acid rain
ignoring the pain of depleted ozone our skins burn as we
take a turn for the worse for there is none to nurse back
the health of our mother that other the earth crumpled
and broken in rubble and ruin the bodies lay strewn
across the battlefield of my immortal soul before my
mind's eye yes i can see the horror the horror now why
can't the surreal reality seduce me and i watch some
more to close your eyes forget what they saw it all can be
stuffed down that hole less who have the most who need
when there's not enough money for one to feed then
comes the malnutrition and i don't feel safe in this world
no i've got to get away from the obscene gore before...it's
too late

His words inspired a sense of awe, fear, and pity in me -all at the same time. They made me forget that I was angry with him. They made me want to understand him. They made me want to read him. They made me want to hold him, just like a good book. As for him, I couldn't tell which emotion was the most powerful at the time: disgust, despair, or delight (in his obvious genius).

Yet, his words bypassed the fact that I was planning to go to a New York state school, Binghamton, in the fall because it was more affordable than a private school. Dwelling on the fact that he hadn't been accepted to a "better" school than Michigan, Chris detailed his disappointment in writing and gave it to me:

his senses raged out at an uncaring, unflinching world

and where do we go from here?

Dear Chris:

We have just completed the review of applicants for the Stanford University class of 1993, and I am very sorry to let you know that we are unable to offer you admission.

and the marines would march on uncaring, unflinching

the sun set, its liquid light, serenely bleeding through the window panes, filled the kitchenette and seemed to drown the Caloric Programmable Micro-Wave in an envelope of blood.

...blood...

BLOOD!

my soul is frozen in the burning ice of jealousy

and what do i do now?

should have applied to other places

at least to Columbia

i really wanna wrestle in college

if you really wanted to wrestle you would have applied to more schools where you could

but i wasn't sure back then, i wasn't sure i wanted to wrestle till around february

i was just too damn LAZY to be bothered with more applications

i didn't really conceive in my mind that i could be rejected

flat out rejected, cold busted

guess that makes me a REJECT

now i can't imagine why Brown would accept me, especially the way i blew off that application

i was too busy

all i could spend my valuable time on was wrestling

and i didn't even win

now there's nothing i can do

nowhere to go

nowhere i can apply that will give me the kind of
education i need as well as the opportunity to grapple

sure i could be a "walk-on" at Michigan, but that's not the
same

i want to be at a place where i'm wanted

where i won't be ignored

inconsequential

a place where someday i could actually contribute to the
team

where i'll have the chance to learn

not just get chucked to the wolves right away

or should i say wolverines

why didn't i listen

why am i such an ass

why are people so stupid

why?

i don't want to go to Rhode Island

i want to LEAVE not just move over

Michigan would be perfect if i could wrestle

if

i feel like screaming

raging

crying

running

running far far away

what am i gonna do with myself

i don't wanna put up with the same shit i've had to deal
with all through high school, the same kinda people and
mentality that permeates New York

Again, as for me, I was staying in New York. That
was a fact he could not see or chose not to see at the time,
which bothered me.

Chapter 20

It was June. We were just about to finish our last year of high school and we were at the Preserve again.

"So, someone's wrong? Aren't they?" I asked, trying to forget, for the time being, about his tirade on his bleak future not that long ago.

"What? Who? Who's wrong?"

"Someone's wrong. We can't all be right... the Christians, the Jews, the Muslims, the atheists... Hey, maybe we're all wrong. How about that?" He didn't say anything, he was still fixated on his more immediate destiny: college. So, after a while I said, "You know what I wish?"

"What?" he asked.

"I wish we could both be there together when we find out what Truth is. Then, we could look in each other's eyes, knowing what's right and what's wrong, and we couldn't argue because it would be fact and not conjecture. We couldn't argue about it anymore."

He still didn't say anything. "And you know what else I wish?" I asked him.

"No, what?"

I was thinking about how this school year would be ending soon, and probably us too. "I wish I could have two lives," I said. "One, so that I could live my own and, another, so that I could observe yours. Yeah, I'd like to be a fly on the wall of your life."

"Well, I'll tell you what," he said, "...if I ever write an autobiography, I'll dedicate it to you."

Our summer together was being cut short because I was going to Spain for three weeks in August. I was going there with the same family that had invited me to France the summer before. It turns out that Michel's in-laws have a place on the Mediterranean and they invited me to visit. On the day before I was to depart, I met Chris for lunch. He'd been working at one of the yacht clubs as a sailing instructor to kids. He hadn't been allowed to go to Nova Scotia that summer on principle; his father said he had to work. To my knowledge, that was the first and only time he was forbidden to spend a summer in Nova Scotia. We bought sandwiches and ate them at the town dock. He said his boss had told him he could take some extra time for lunch, so we walked to his house; it was about fifteen minutes away.

We went up the stairs;

We went into his room,

and fell onto the floor.

I wore a green cotton sundress that day.

It buttoned down the middle,

and up the middle.

Chris left the room for a moment. I heard classical music coming from downstairs. Chris came back in again. Then, much later, he went back to work.

I arrived home to find flowers had arrived before me: a dozen red roses with one white iris in the middle, towering over the roses. They were from Chris. Then, I was on a plane to Spain.

Chapter 21

When I came home from Spain, I brought a whole lot of stuff back with me for Chris. I brought back Spanish comic books, a leather hat, a T-shirt and a cane. I brought Chris a cane because he had had knee surgery during my absence. I spread everything all over his kitchen table. Chris said he liked the comic books the best. I still get embarrassed every time I think about it. I didn't know what to get him. I didn't want to get the wrong thing; so, I got everything. Why did I care so much about his opinion?

In his kitchen, I stood wearing a black skirt -a black long and full skirt. I wore black espadrilles that I had picked up in Spain for just three dollars. I wore a black lycra top. I wore the sleeves of it off my shoulders, without a bra underneath. I was very tan and my hair was long and curly. He gave me a hug, and as he had his arms around me, I hung my head back and told him that I hadn't paid for one drink the entire three weeks.

"Not one?"

I didn't answer. I just smiled. He had missed me. I could see that. He took me into the living room. He didn't lead me to the couch; he led me to the floor. Once I was lying on the floor, he walked over to the stereo and put on a French album I never knew they had, or could ever recognize again if I were to hear it. He pulled my skirt up gently, kissing my thighs. Then, he kissed my neck for a while until he moved to my shoulders. He kissed my bare shoulders. He knew. He always made love to the clothes I was wearing. He was careful to leave them on just long enough, take them off just slowly enough, or not take them off at all. This time, he didn't take off my skirt.

Chapter 22

Sometime before we said goodbye that summer, I sat on my back porch and wrote these words on green sheets of paper:

Dear Chris,

Throughout these four years of high school, you have been close and dear to my heart. Our friendship is one discovery that I'll never regret having made. You have made me open up to you and share so much with you that I would have otherwise kept all to myself. Looking through your mind's eye, my view of the world and of people has been broadened.

I've never known anyone like you and I know I never will again, but that's because you're an individual with your own mind. Your individuality is a trait of great value; treasure it always. You're a person with principles. I admire and respect that very much. Please don't ever compromise them so long as you believe in them. You're a person who believes in free expression. Don't ever resist an impulse or be in any way reserved. Share your thoughts and ideas, and most of all, yourself, with the world; for, a person's individuality depends upon the expression of one's mind.

The color green will always remind me of you because it's nature's color and because you hold so dear to your heart all of that which it has to offer. Your love for nature is one of the things I most admire about you. I hope that you will always preserve within your heart an appreciation for nature's beauty and pleasures.

There's so much about you that's warm and wonderful. There's so much about you that needs to be shared with the rest of the world, and, of course, there's so much of the world for you to explore and experience. Always remember to enjoy life to its fullest. I'm giving you a copy of "Iris," so that you may read it, enjoy it, and reread it. I want you to see the notes that you made in the margins and the parts you chose to underline. I hope that you will never stop thinking. Never let a word, whether spoken or written, slip by without digesting its meaning. Never cease to wonder or to be amazed, and don't ever stop questioning those things in this world that are puzzling and intriguing to the mind.

I've mentioned once before that I have a wish; that wish is to somehow live two lives simultaneously: one, so that I can live my own life, and another, so that I can observe yours. However much an impossibility it is, it would please me to do this because, you, your ideas, your ways, intrigue me. I'm extremely curious to see how you will live your life and what accomplishments you will make. I have confidence in you that you will "succeed" at whatever it is you choose to do as long as you continue to be determined and persevere. Never lose sight of that which is important to you, the goals that you have, and those that you will set for yourself in the future.

I have another wish and that is to find all the answers to all the questions that I have -to figure the whole world out one day. If ever that were to happen, somehow, somewhere, I'd wish that you'd be there too. I'd want you to be there because, so often, I've talked to you about this and because, if everything were explained, we wouldn't differ at all in our views. We could discuss what is, rather than what might be. I believe that the reason you interest me so much is that you've challenged my mind and my views. Nobody ever did that before. We've had many different opinions, but I believe that our differences made it possible for me to grow and to change -to broaden my perspective of the world. I'm glad that you are who you are. I'd never want you to be any different. I'll always be glad to have had the opportunity to have known you. You've taught me a lot about people -how they act and how they should act. You may not realize this, but you demand and receive a great deal of respect and admiration from everyone -most of all, me. You're a great person and people love you for that. You're a person who has character. You most definitely are not shallow at all. You're a sensitive person who cares for others. You're an honest and open person with a kind heart and warm smile.

I want you to know how much I appreciate all that you have shared with me about yourself. I am glad that you shared your writing and your interest in books, especially comic books (Calvin & Hobbes). I always like to see the sparkle in your eyes and excitement in your face when you talk about something that really interests you and that you really enjoy. I hope that you will enjoy the art class you have decided to take at Michigan next year.

We've spent so many hours together in the past few years that the memories are numerous; and they are impossible to recount. We took many walks together and had many talks. We laughed a lot together too. Thank you. Thank you for the warmth of your hugs and touch.

I'll think of you next year when I'm sitting in my Human Evolution class because you are the reason that I am taking the course -you made me curious.

I want you to know that I will forever be your friend; if you need someone, I'm here. My ears and arms are always open for you. I want to wish you all the luck in the world. I hope that you will be a happy person - always.

Although others are comfortable,
Although others are complacent,
With the warm air that surrounds them-
With the warm air that suffocates them,
Though others shiver from the cold-
From the wind of the outside world,
Reach out; open every window;
Feel the invigorating breeze.
I know that you want to change the world,
And if it's at all a triumph,
You should know that you have changed mine.

My memory of you will never fade. I will remember you for a long, long time. There will always be a special place in my heart for you.

"Fare thee well! and if forever,
Still forever, fare thee well."

-Byron

Made in the USA
Lexington, KY
08 February 2019